Grandparents Run in the Family

By Yvette Jean Silver

P
PINNACLE BOOKS

PINNACLE BOOKS are published by

Kensington Publishing Corp.
850 Third Avenue
New York, NY 10022

The P logo Reg U.S. Pat. & TM Off. Pinnacle is a trademark of Kensington Publishing Corp.

First Printing: September, 1995

ISBN: 0-7860-0181-X
Printed in the United States of America

In memory of my grandmother,
Jean Silver.

Thanks to my parents, Martin and Denise Silver, and to my brother Dan, for their love and support. Special thanks to Lynn Seligman and Paul Dinas for making this book possible.

CONGRATULATIONS! YOU'RE A GRANDFATHER.

THAT MUST MAKE YOU THE GRANDMOTHER.

THERE'S SOMEONE WHO WANTS TO MEET YOU.

GO AHEAD AND GET ACQUAINTED,

DO SOME BONDING.

YOU ALREADY HAVE SO MUCH IN COMMON . . .

LIKE YOUR HAIRSTYLES

AND YOUR FAVORITE PASTIMES.

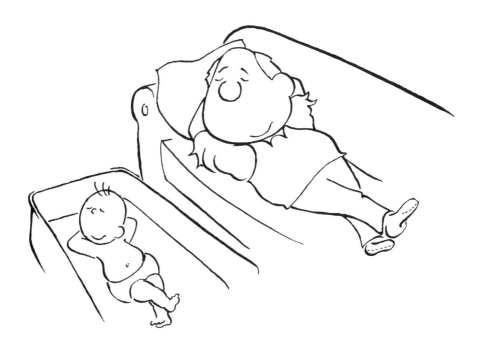

YOUR LOVE OF PAMPERING

AND YOUR INSATIABLE CURIOSITY.

AND TO CERTAIN PEOPLE.

AND THE ENDLESS SEARCH FOR THE PERFECT NAME,

OR THEREABOUTS.

YOU WORKED HOURS MAKING AN AUTHENTIC HEIRLOOM,

BABYPROOFING FROM FLOOR TO CEILING,

AND GETTING UP TO SPEED ON THE LATEST IN VIDEO EQUIPMENT.

AND WHEN THE DAY FINALLY ARRIVED,

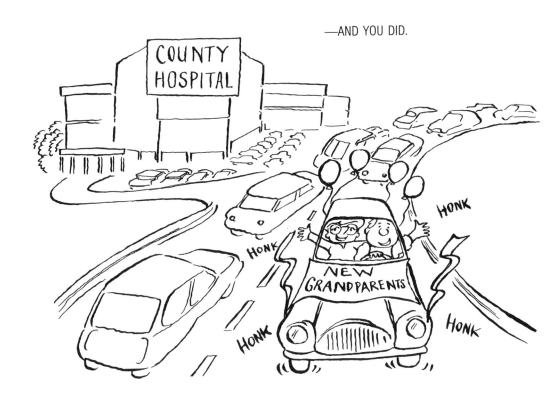

INTO BONAFIDE PARENTS.

THEY FINALLY UNDERSTAND WHAT YOU HAD TO
GO THROUGH RAISING THEM,

WAITING FOR THE DAY THEY'D MAKE IT UP TO YOU.

WHEN IT REALLY COUNTS, IT'S YOU THEY TURN TO.

EVEN THOUGH YOU'D GLADLY DROP ANYTHING AT THE CHANCE.

WHO COULD RESIST SUCH A FACE . . .

OR SUCH A SCENT . . .

OR SUCH SOUNDS?

AND SHOULD THE LITTLE ONE START TO MISS MOMMY AND DADDY,

YOU'RE ALWAYS THE NEXT BEST THING.

YOU'LL FIND THAT SO MUCH ABOUT BABIES HAS CHANGED
FROM WHAT YOU REMEMBER.

THE PREPARATION:

THEN

NOW

THE LABOR:

THE NECESSITIES:

THEN   NOW

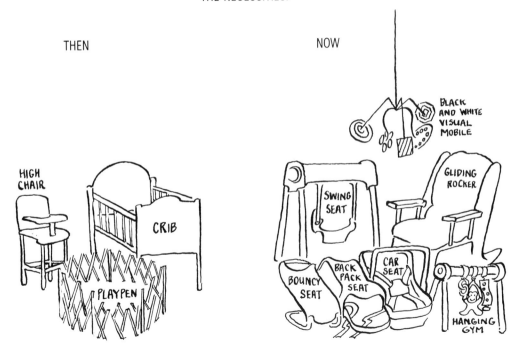

THE DIAPERS:

THEN

NOW

THE MODES OF TRANSPORTATION:

THEN

NOW

THE MOMS:

THEN

NOW

THE FASHIONS:

THEN

NOW

AND, OF COURSE, THE GRANDPARENTS:

THEN   NOW

WHEN IT COMES TO THE QUESTION OF FAMILY RESEMBLANCE,

THERE ARE MANY OPINIONS,

BUT ONLY ONE OPINION MATTERS.

TO GET UP AND GO WHEREVER YOUR HEART DESIRES.

BUT OF ALL THE WORLD'S WONDERFUL PLACES,

THERE'S JUST ONE PLACE YOU REALLY WANT TO BE.

WHEN EVERYONE IS TRYING TO GET YOU TO SLOW DOWN,

GRANDCHILDREN BELIEVE YOU CAN STILL DO ANYTHING.

TO THEM, AGE IS JUST THE NUMBER OF CANDLES ON YOUR CAKE,

WRINKLES ARE WHAT YOU GET FROM BEING IN THE BATH,

CHUBBY CHEEKS ARE MUCH BETTER FOR CUDDLING,

AND YOUR "SPECIAL" TEETH CAN ONLY MEAN THAT YOU KNOW
THE TOOTH FAIRY PERSONALLY.

IN THE YEARS TO COME, NO MATTER WHEN YOU CALL,

THERE'LL ALWAYS BE SOMEONE WHO CAN'T WAIT TO TALK TO YOU.

SOMEONE WHO SHARES YOUR EXQUISITE TASTE.

SOMEONE WHO THINKS EVEN YOUR OLD STANDBYS ARE THE BEST.

AND WHO SEES THE GENIUS IN "THE THREE STOOGES."

THERE'S NOTHING LIKE GRANDCHILDREN TO ATTRACT EXTRA ATTENTION,

TO CURE WHAT AILS YOU,

AT YOUR HOUSE, THEY DON'T ALWAYS HAVE TO FOLLOW THE RULES

ONLY TO GET SPOILED BACK.

AND JUST WHEN YOU START TO WONDER WHERE YOU'RE GETTING
THE ENERGY FOR ALL THIS . . .

THEY SOMEHOW KNOW TO NAP.

IN BECOMING A GRANDPARENT, YOU'VE JOINED A SPECIAL CLUB

AND NEW RESPONSIBILITIES.

SHYNESS IS OUT.

RERUNS ARE IN.

OR TO GO A LITTLE OVERBOARD.

EVERYTHING THEY DO MAKES YOU PROUD.

ISN'T IT WONDERFUL THAT . . .